MINE TO CLAIM

DESPERATELY DEPRAVED
BOOK 1

WHIT LAVONNE

© Whit LaVonne 2024

Cover by @evertein_c

All rights reserved. No part of this book may be reproduced or used in any manner without the prior written permission of the copyright owner, except for the use of brief quotations in a book review.

This author does not support AI.

To anyone who likes to get a little wild.

AUTHOR'S NOTE

I can't believe you're actually reading this page right now, thank you for choosing to pick up my debut book!

As a Detroit author, I recognize that the land I live on is stolen. I want to acknowledge that this book was written on the contemporary and ancestral homelands of the three Anishinaabe nations of the council of Three Fires: Ojibwe (Chippewa), Odawa (Ottawa), and Bodewatomi (Potawatomi) peoples. Indigenous communities, both here and beyond, continue to be systemically excluded and oppressed; I stand in solidarity with them.

I know I'm supposed to save the thank yous for the end, but this is my book and I do what I want! Thank you to my editors, Brittany and Miranda. They both pushed me to become a better writer during this process; any remaining fault in this book is my own. Thank you to my sensitivity readers, who provided thorough and constructive feedback.

Though I do my best to continue my education and support of marginalized groups, I am not and will never be perfect. As a Black woman in America, there are many struggles I can relate to, as well as privileges I benefit from. My intent is never to speak over other marginalized groups, but to celebrate them. I want my books to reflect the beautiful and diverse world I live in, whenever possible, and strive to include people and perspectives from all walks of life. However, if you see space for me to grow, or are in some way harmed by my work, and would like to speak further, please contact me here: heyitswhitlavonne@gmail.com

Furthermore, I am honored to share that 10% of profits from this book will be donated to The Arctic Rose Foundation, an organization that works to support Northern Inuit, First Nations, and Metis youth, indefinitely. I encourage you to do your own research on MMIW and the Land Back movement; you can also find more information on The Arctic Rose Foundation here: https://arcticrose.org/

Lastly, I want to include some content warnings for you.

Mild- vomit, anxious thoughts, family planning (in epilogue)

Moderate- toxic ex, bullying (off page, historical), mental and emotional abuse (off page, historical), dementia in a parent

Tropes- fated mates, omegaverse, fish out of water, "touch *HIM* and die"

Kinks- somnophilia, anal, adult toy use, public play, breeding (no baby)

Tags- primal, territorial

More in depth information can be found on my website: whitlavonne.com

————

These aliens are looking for refuge... and mates. Would you deny them?

Lance

Living in Alaska has brought me closer to my roots, but also keeps me rooted in the same small town as my toxic ex-girlfriend.

A trip to Cancun, Mexico is starting to look like the perfect breath of fresh air. But when I meet a girl on the beach who says we're mates, things start to get a little weird.

And that's not all; she says she's from outer space and was sent to Earth along with twenty-nine other aliens to await her planet's rebirth.

Talk about an unforgettable vacation.

Georgia

Being a beta in a lycan pack isn't as glamorous as it looks. Especially when you're the runt of a pack living on a planet experiencing the Great Mating Ceasement. It makes me unnecessary, insignificant, a throwaway.

But on Earth, I can be more than that. So when the opportunity arises, I say to hell with my pack and make a break for it.

I thought hours of pawing through forest floors were in my future; who knew I would actually find a mate, would actually be *worthy* of one.

Now all I have to do is keep him.

"Mine to Claim" is the first book of the Desperately Depraved series following a pod of refugee aliens searching for connection on Earth. It's great for Kimberly Lemming

and Ruby Dixon readers, as well as anyone looking for something short and spicy. This novella contains adult language and sex scenes. Please see the author's website for content warnings.

PROLOGUE

Dear Valued Citizen of the Yorgürrian Conduct,

We are all so honored to be a part of the Yorgürr's twenty-ninth burn and rebirth cycle! Your patience during the lean times of the preceding decay cycle has been responsible for the unprecedented success across various Yorgürrian industries. We know sacrifice is difficult, but the more we give during the decay, the greater our best and brightest can make our planet's rebirth!

We appreciate your patience with planet-wide rations, energy blackouts, and droughts as all additional funding has been streamlined to support our best scientists. As you know, they have been working tirelessly to prepare adequate medications, modifications, and accommodations for each citizen, scattered across several galaxies while we await the rebirth of our home.

We, the Yorgürrian Conduct, are now ready to

formally declare your planet assignment: You will be awaiting the rebirth of Yorgürr on planet Earth, Galaxy 4D2 in Quadrant 6. Please proceed to the location at the date and time stated below to receive your modifications to blend in with Earth inhabitants along with the proper medications to prepare you for your travel. As a reminder, all citizens will receive one shot of malgdemahn to help them sleep during cosmic travel, and additional doses will be provided on board your podship should you need them.

The Great Mating Ceasement has echoed through generations of Yorgürrians for decades now. The Yorgürrian Conduct encourages you to seek a mating, if and when possible, on your assigned planet. Any mated species, and kits, will be permitted to journey back with full Yorgürrian citizenship and coverage should they choose to do so.

Remember,

Your government loves you.
Your government believes in you.
Your government fights for you.
Yongda!

CHAPTER 1
GEORGIA

IT'S HOT, and the nerves in my fingers tingle. They say that's normal when you wake up from cryo-sleep and seventeen days of space travel. I roll my neck and turn my head side to side, then crack open my eyes. The tube I'm in has a gray, semi-transparent viewing window through which I can only see fuzzy blobs. The built-in privacy protections keep others from clearly seeing me, but also keep me from clearly seeing outside. I strain my ears but can't hear anything more than a soft *shwim shwim* of the air tank connected to my cryo-tube. I take a few more moments to rub some feeling back into my arms and hands before leaving to see how my fellow travelers are faring.

Space travel was not what I'd pictured it would be. Maybe that's because I slept most of the way here, but unlike many other passengers on this podship, I didn't have that spark of hope that usually comes with traveling to a new place.

The constant giddy laughter, bets, and predictions filling the cabin two days after our departure eventually felt like daggers to my eardrums and exhausted the last of my patience. So I'd taken an extra shot of *malgdemahn* to increase my drowsiness and slipped away to the sleeping tanks when my pack wasn't paying attention.

I could've pretended to be as excited as the orc, Caesephalana, or even as apprehensive as Nikquale, who usually takes the form of blue-gray mist on Yorgürr. But that would've been too much effort, and I've always been one to take things a day at a time; as a beta, it's one of the first pack lessons I learned.

The second lesson is that there's no time like the present, so I take a steadying breath and push the button to open my cryo-tube. Snores of heavy slumber greet me, and I remove my outermost shirt layer to adjust to the temperature, taking in the sleeping status of those in the main cabin. The angels in our traveling group, Heiere and Terrerrin, sit to my left on a large sleeping pillow, arms hugging, legs tangled, with Heirere's head tipped back and mouth open. I'm not sure how Terrerrin sleeps so soundly next to his grisly refrain. How can any of my fellow Lycans continue to sleep piled on the ground along with several other travelers?

As I inspect the rest of the room, my question is answered. Empty alcohol bottles are strewn along the main cabin floor. No doubt they all drank themselves into a stupor after partying for the first time in maybe two years.

Ever since we'd learned our pod would head out to a planet called Earth, our alpha has made training everyone's top priority. None of the omegas in our pack have been bred in years, lowering our status as a group. Everyone's hoping we find our pack's one true mate while we're planetside and be able to take kits home when Yorgürr is ready.

We've studied and trained for how to survive and protect a potential mate in the diverse geography Earth offers. Well, everyone else in the pack trained. Since I'm the runt beta of the pack, Alpha deemed me the punching bag. While everyone else was learning offensive and defensive attacks, I got great at blocking. I had hoped that with the strict training, the leaders of our pack were moving away from the practice of wasting nights away on drinks, but this just proves that they're back to their old habits.

The partying, plus the initial shot of *malgdemahn* we all received before departure, means that they're probably knocked out cold for a while. I'll have some time to explore on my own.

I step over bottles, smoke containers, empty food canisters, and clothing, careful not to wake anyone prematurely, but almost trip over Jurrae's tentacles when I notice that the podship door is already open.

I conduct a quick headcount of all the other Lycans. One... two... three... eight... No one else from my pack is awake, so someone else opened the door. I consider shoving Jurrae's wayward limbs to the side but think better of it. He doesn't like others touching him, even if it's to help. I shrug; if he gets stepped on by someone else later, I'm sure Garrekth, our pod's nurse, will help him.

I push the rest of the way through the pod door and stop in my tracks. Earth. The ground is white as far as the eye can see. I'm hesitant to move, and look back at the bodies piled on the floor in the pod. I scrunch up my nose, decided.

The first step onto Earth is peace. True peace. The white stuff is resistant at first, but then my feet sink into a soft, pillowy hole. A chill zings up through my uncovered toes, all the way up my legs and spine. Even though we studied this planet, it's nothing like I imagined. The wind whistles through my hair, and I take a deep breath, chilled air filling my lungs. An unfamiliar scent fills my nose—this feels good.

I think I might fall in love with this planet way before I ever fall in love with one of its inhabitants.

I catch the scent of smoke, and it distracts me from the thrilling chill at my feet. Mazg, Johran, and Frank sit around a small fire, huddled together. Of course they would have to ruin this beautiful experience with Mazg's belly fire, but, being a dragon and two tlakatl respectively, I can't really fault them.

I smile at how similar and yet distinct this two-legged form looks on Mazg compared to his dragon form. His eyes are the same emerald green as his scales, and his curly hair looks just as soft as his wings seemed to be in his true form. Johran and Frank both have angular faces here, and I can't make out any more details of their form because blankets cover the rest of their bodies. It looks like their need for heat has transferred over to these new forms.

Mazg and I both have curly hair, but where his is dark, mine is auburn, and the twins' are both a pale yellow. My curls are big enough to bounce while Mazg's are tiny and coil close to his head. Johran's hair is wavy and Frank's hair is the straightest out of all of us. Where Frank and Johran's skin is a warm beige, mine is a light bronze, and Mazg's is a rich brown. Mazg's nose is wider, and Johran and I both have little skin spots dashed across our faces.

It makes me excited to see what other distinctions these humans can have; and, if I'm lucky enough to find a mate, what will they look like?

"Hey, how long have you guys been awake?" I'm careful not to get too close to the fire they huddle around, preferring instead to dig my toes further into the cold, white ground and let the wind carry my voice.

"Two fractal days on this blasted planet. I'm not sure yet how they measure time here, but we've only seen one new light here so far," Frank yells over to me. His fraternal twin, Johran, stands next to him, bundled, teeth chattering.

"You can stop with the pitying looks, Gjourshe," Mazg says over his shoulder. "We're cold and miserable, but we'll only be here long enough for my wings to warm up. They froze beneath this shifted form, but they're almost ready. I can smell a warmer climate on the winds. We'll be getting out of here soon."

Ever the planner, of course, Mazg already has a way out. If he were in a better mood, I bet he would've chuckled at the twins with some quick remark like, "A dragon doesn't shiver, one simply... dances." But apparently this temperature is severe enough to bother even one of his kind. But getting out of here? Mazg is known as a team player, a leader. I'd often wished I could be a part of his pack instead —if dragons ever had packs.

I creep closer to the fire. "What about the others? What if they don't wake up before you're ready to leave? Would you really go without everyone?"

"How do we guarantee we can make it in these temperatures until then? These temperatures may be fine for some of the others, but you know we won't be able to last like this," Frank says.

"But—"

"We're on a new planet," Johnran's gravelly voice adds. "No safety net, no rules. Between diplomacy and survival, you have to choose the latter."

"Which is why we need to relocate somewhere warmer." Mazg turns to me. "There's enough room on my back for three. You could go with us."

I shift on my feet.

"I wouldn't want to pressure you away from your pack," he continues, "but you're good people. If you'd like to leave with us, we'd love to have you."

"Don't make any decisions now," Frank adds. "Maybe wait and see if your pack wakes up in time first. But I second Mazg. We'd love to have you with us." Frank looks back to Johran, who nods his agreement.

"Okay, thanks. I'll think about it," I lie and move away from the fire to lie on the cold, crunchy ground. I almost sink past the surface and become surrounded by the small, soft nuggets of white, praying to every goddess I can think of. If my pack slumbers long enough for Mazg's wings to thaw out, there'll be no one to stop me from riding on the back of a dragon, coasting through winds that taste a lot like freedom. No "thinking about it" required.

The sky darkens as I await my fate, and small twinkling lights appear. Mazg tells the others that these are stars in the Earth's galaxy, tiny dying gatherings of plasma that shine every night.

It makes me think of Yorgürr and the fate of our people. Did everyone make it off the planet in time? Has it exploded yet? How are the other pods of citizens faring on their temporary planets? Has Sylvxria woken up yet?

I smile at the memory of my best friend. Sylvxria and I daydreamed every day while moving shipments in the Twynsoind factory we both worked for. "Gjourshe, this could be the start of a new life, for both of us," she'd tell me every morning. By the afternoon, she'd always have me convinced that maybe, just maybe, it could be. I chuckle to myself remembering how I had to repeat her spiel back to her after her government modification surgery. Her tall antenna had morphed into two nubs on her forehead to better blend in with the organisms of the planet she was being sent to, and she'd hated it! On Yorgürr, her antenna had been a sign of beauty, but on her assigned planet, everyone there looks exactly the same and tells each other apart by a magnetic chip they're given at birth or upon landing.

As the wind turns blessedly colder, I wonder how *my* looks will be received here.

Lost in thought, I'm not paying attention to the boys as they continue to make plans and only recognize that they've moved away from the fire when I hear the *crunch, crunch, crunch* of the ground. Soon Mazg is leaning over me on two legs, his sinewy wings flared out proudly and a manic grin on his face.

"It's time, Gjourshe. Have you made your choice?"

I glance back at the podship and take in a big sniff; my pack slumbers, and everything in me wants to leave, but I'm still nervous. I don't hide the skepticism in my voice when I ask, "How are you going to carry us? I thought you could shift?"

But then Mazg steps back, that grin turning into a full-toothed smile as a green shimmer dashes across him. "Who said I couldn't?"

CHAPTER 2
LANCE

DO you ever want to stick your head into a pot of boiling cow balls? I don't make a habit of it, but on this crisp morning, sitting around the table with my friends at Aunt Bob's diner, that's exactly what I want to do. Finn has just asked me how things are going with my toxic ex.

Nothing could be worse than coming clean about how I still allow her in my life when I've told them multiple times, at this very table, that I would cut her out of it completely. But then I'm saved when Josh gives his signature belly laugh from across the table and starts passing his phone around so everyone can see the new viral video on TamFam, and Finn's question is quickly forgotten.

I already know what they would've said.

"Lance, install that back door lock and stop holding onto the idea of her once and for all."

They might have even dragged me down to the hardware store on Mulberry Lane if they knew about what happened this morning. Especially since they had to all but drag me the first time to change the front door.

My uneaten waffles sit in front of me, bordered by the

gleam of the silver rings on my hands while I think back to when I got my first basket of fresh blueberry muffins a week after our breakup, just sitting on the counter with no note but obviously from *her*. I figured it was a friendly gesture to show me that we could be civil. I was wrong.

Right now, Mary Galdstein is likely somewhere with her gaggle of girlfriends, touching up her red nails, droning on about how I'm sure to "come crawling back to her" any minute now. She's probably already told the story at least twenty times today of how she snuck into my backyard, used the spare key under the rug to open the back door, and left blueberry muffins on the counter for me with a note saying "Have a good day 'at work.'"

Well, she probably told a romanticized version of it that left out the context that "at work" was a jab at me. I'd told her in our last big fight that looking for a better-paying job was working in itself. And when I'm trying to finish oil painting commissions, it's not a good use of my time. That same argument was where she'd said, in that shrill tone of hers, "Everyone can see how you don't deserve me. It makes you look like a washed-up loser, and when you realize no one else wants you, you'll know where to find me."

"Hey, Lance," Oran calls from the other side of the table, "Garrett and I are planning to go for another hike the weekend after next. Do you want to come?"

If it were just Oran, I would usually say no. He loves to change his mind at the last minute, choose the most difficult route regardless of our supplies or lack thereof, and isn't always as careful as I'd like him to be. But with Garrett going, he'll reel it in; his boyfriend usually brings out the best in him.

"Yeah, just let me know what time." I realize too late that I don't even know where I just agreed to hike.

When we first started dating, I would do the same thing with Mary, naively saying yes and figuring out the rest just to be near her. We both enjoyed hiking and watching the Northern Lights, so I thought we could work out. She'd been nicer then, bringing me pastries from Tim's Barrel of Bits bakery—the family business her father had built from scratch—for breakfast so I wouldn't have to eat Nutri-Grain bars all the time.

But none of that was worth being with someone who tried to mold me to fit their lifestyle instead of appreciating me for who I am. In hindsight, I should've never asked her out in the first place, especially when every person in my small friend group here in Noatak, Alaska, warned me that she's a manipulator and a people-user. I should've kept my focus on my goals, my reason for moving here.

"Hey, you gonna finish those?" Tom asks beside me. I look down at my waffles again, the syrup long since soaked in. I should've known I would not eat them now that winter has passed and the anxious need to bulk up and ride out the weather is over.

I slide my plate in front of him and lean back against the round booth seat. "No, man. Have at it."

Roughing it out in the cold and making it through the sunless winters can prove to folks that they're stronger than they know, and as much as it makes me proud to be one of them, I came up here from North Carolina to learn more about my ancestors—the Inuit. My mother's dementia is progressing, but before the doctors and the tests and the tears, she used to tell me stories. Stories passed down from her mother's mother —a line of beautiful people with an extensive history, locked safely away in the blood flowing through my veins.

I wanted more of that, always have; especially after

pockets of time started slipping away for her. So three years ago, I sold my home and rental properties and moved up here to get reunited with the land and community. And strangely, I feel more connected to my mother here than when I'm right in front of her.

The conversation around the table has long since moved on without me, but I try to snap out of my melancholic thoughts as the boys and I stand to say our goodbyes. We part ways, and I head over to the Main Street General Store. The bell above the door rings, and I'm greeted with the familiar scent of leather and peanuts.

"Hey, Lance!" Parker shouts over the aisles. His dad lets him work the storefront on the days he wants to skip school. So here he is, currently testing his free throw skills with each peanut shell he tosses into the trash can.

"Hey, Parks, how's life?" I ask over the short aisles. I peruse the store's new items; some spring-related magnets and buttons, hunting knives and... cheeseburger-flavored chips?

"It's all right. Mrs. Kranger's as strict as ever, but I'll manage."

"One more year of high school, right? Do your best and the rest will come."

He nods in response and dips his head, likely reaching for another peanut.

I make my way to the dairy section to grab some milk and eggs. Mama didn't raise no fool, and she'd be ashamed if she learned I had the makings of a blueberry crumble in my kitchen and let it go to waste. After all, I'm just one person; I can't eat all the muffins Mary dropped off by myself, and if I share them with the guys as-is, I'll never hear the end of it. Tim's bakery houses the best blueberry muffins in a hundred-mile radius. They'll know where, and exactly *who*, the muffins came from.

Cringing at the embarrassment I hope to avoid, I scratch at the scruff on my jaw and decidedly reach for oat milk, remembering that the last time I tried almond it did *not* go well.

Something bright yellow catches my eye from the bulletin board beside me. A promotional card with a yellow beach umbrella stuck firmly in the sand and the words "The Ocean Awaits" in bold, white letters hangs from its pin. "Cancún, México" is printed at the bottom; no other words are needed to sell the idea of a beautiful beach vacation.

And, for the first time in weeks, with an ex I've been trying to distance myself from, I've finally found my breathing room.

CHAPTER 3
GEORGIA

YOU KNOW those winds of freedom I mentioned? They're more like the turbulence of tragedy. After the hours it took to let Mazg's wings finish unthawing, the twins and I saddled up between the spikes on Mazg's back and took off. And it was only then that I realized a Lycan is meant to keep her four paws on the ground; and from the amount of times the twins have barfed, I'm not the only one with that sentiment.

Mazg flew us over water as long as his tired and under-used wings could take us before touching down on land in a scorching, humid place. If I'd known that we'd travel so far away from the cold, white ground, I would've asked to pull over and savor it some more. The deep cold of it was absolutely delicious. But I know the others all need this warmer weather, and I'd rather be with them than my pack, so I keep quiet.

"We've been walking for days," Frank says into the wind. "Are we there yet?"

We probably don't make the best traveling partners, as I

need breaks from the big, burning star in the sky, and the twins are lethargic without it. But Mazg is patient and makes sure we all stay together and get where we are going in one piece. I compare him to our alpha, Elloyt, who would've left me in the dust the second I couldn't keep up... I'm once again grateful for this opportunity to get away from my pack.

"Almost," Mazg replies. "Let's keep moving."

Mazg is calm and collected, leading our small group through the hot, humid land. Tall stems sprout from the ground, providing shade and fruit. The packed ground also provides vegetation and homes for other animals.

We pass by several large structures and get our first real look at Earth's primary inhabitants—the humans—from afar, but we keep moving. His dragon nose is strong, even more so than mine, so we continue to follow him as he's said he's leading us to a large gathering on the other side of the peninsula.

For the umpteenth time today, I stare at another round, pink fruit hanging from one of the tall stems we pass by. It looks edible, but we don't know what the culture and customs are here, so we haven't picked or hunted anything yet.

Besides, we were prepared to survive for quite a while before our first feeding on Earth thanks to all the loads of pills, vitamins, and genetically-enhanced herbs thrust our way from the Yorgürrian government and scientists, so we can still wait a while to eat. Dragons and tlakatl hardly ever know what it is to hunger as they are the darlings of society, but this may be the first time I have truly been physically satiated and content in my lifetime, and so we are united in our top priority—finding the mateable inhabitants of Earth.

"I still don't understand why we can't just go to a

smaller gathering. I've scouted humans in almost every new light," Johran grumbles just like he has every day since we made it to land.

"I know it's frustrating," Mazg says over his shoulder, "but we don't know if these humans are the same or what relationships or policies they have. It's best to get ourselves situated in a densely populated area so we can learn as much as possible, as quickly as possible. Plus, it'll make it easier for us to blend in when we're in a larger crowd and give our chips more opportunities to take in the languages spoken here."

The star still bakes down on us as we continue our march, and eight new lights later, we finally reach the location Mazg decided on.

What seems like hundreds of humans bustle down aisles, their voices rising to combine into one mumbled roar of movement, and I'm feeling overwhelmed. After a life spent in one pack, in one home, on one planet, we're actually here on Earth getting ready to mingle with humans.

Johran ducks behind a large, panel-covered structure filled with woven baskets. Already, we can see humans milling about, trading things for small disks and gesturing wildly.

"This is it. Down there is our future," Mazg says, breaking the pregnant silence between the four of us.

This could be the start of a new life. I let Sylvxria's words bolster my resolve and hope. I can do this.

"Here's the plan," he continues. "As long as it pleases us, we move as a group. If it no longer does, we let the others know that we'll be off on our own." He receives quiet nods from all of us, each thinking about the possibilities right here in front of us.

"Well, if that's settled then—" Frank drifts around the

structure we've been hiding behind and walks into the throng with Mazg and Johran following closely.

Here goes nothing. I take a deep breath. *My future awaits.*

CHAPTER 4
GEORGIA

Pollo
Shoes
Mantequillas
Maiale
Cesta

A MARKET—*UN* *mercado*—we are in the middle of a market.

The smells and sounds of the market assault me as we get closer to the beautiful chaos of a community of people supporting each other. Kits are running, chasing, laughing, crying. Some humans mosey while others dash quickly between stalls—haggling and gesturing before finalizing a trade. Food is sizzling on hot stones, hanging from stall roofs and sitting in barrels, baskets, and carts. Hot oil puffs pastries that get filled with shredded meat covered in spices that waft a tantalizing scent around us.

The translator chip hasn't completed downloading this

language yet, as it prioritizes words we hear over the words we want, so I don't know if Mexico is the name of this market, land mass, or the human's name for Earth.

Either way, I'm happy to know what to call that crunchy rolled dough filled with cheese—*marquesitas*. Frank has already convinced a kind woman to give him five, which he shares with Johran and me, but I do imagine we'll need to find some of those small disks—*dinero*—to trade with soon.

With my stomach full, I continue down the main aisle of the market toward a driving, melodic sound. Four men in wide, colorful hats play a collection of instruments in the street—*mariachi*. One man steps forward, his red and black hat sits low on his brow, and he sings.

"Ay que hermosura de mujer he conocido."

Children dance, turning and swaying, laughing as they swing their arms while adults clap along. The man continues to sing of a woman, his treasure, and how much he loves her. Couples join the dancing as he sings about giving his heart away to his love.

I can't help but smile and stomp my feet when he sings of kissing her, and I think about what it might be like to kiss a mate as I dance along. The images the chip pulls up are a little foreign to me but, with a mate, I'm sure just about anything will be fun. Two more songs entrance the crowd before the mariachi band takes a break and I continue exploring the stalls.

Later, I find Mazg between two fruit stalls. He's staring at the produce, probably hoping to hear the names as people make transactions, but he doesn't look up to see the lady behind the stall staring at him.

I can't blame her. His deep brown skin and curly hair that reaches up toward the sky stands out amongst the throng of pink, beige, and golden-brown people who fill the space. It seems his features garner attention, and I say a little thank you to the goddess, because after years of being the butt of the joke, that attention is *not* for me.

In fact, none of this is for me. The people hustle and bustle without an alpha in sight—selling, buying, eating, making. "*El sol*" beats down (apparently that's what they call the big light in the sky) and all around we are met with water. This is nothing like our home planet.

Did you really think you could come out here without your pack and survive? the self-doubt taunts. *I bet the pack is glad you're gone. Clumsy little Gjourshe, silly little Gjourshe. I bet they were hoping you'd be the one who didn't wake up in time. You're dead weight to anyone around you.* It's easier to ignore the insults of others, but it's harder when the words come from my own brain.

New words in new languages continue to fly past me as I signal to the twins that I'm leaving the area and follow the main path out of the market. I just need to get away for a moment so that stupid little voice in my head can shut its stupid little mouth.

I pass by large... *hotels*, with *cars*, and *buses*, and people until I come to a... *beach*. My curiosity about the Earth's different grounds may never end. This ground, the *sand*, is just a warmer version of the... hmm, that's weird. The chip isn't downloading a word for the white ground I saw when I first left the ship.

The gripping fear that my chip might already malfunction tries to overtake me, but the sound of the waves drowns it out. They're calming, comforting, these waves; and even more so when I stare at them. The light of the sun shimmers on the surface. The foam of each crash invites me closer, and I sync my breath with the ebb and flow of them.

I don't know how many hours pass as I stare into the ocean's dance, wiggling my toes in the sand, when the purest, most tantalizing mix of banafang trees and juliptic—a soft fabric usually used for blankets and made from the leaves of juliptous bushes back home—arrests my nose.

Mate.

CHAPTER 5
LANCE

THE PAST FOUR days have been amazing. Cave and ruin tours, great food and drinks, and the beach have been exactly what I needed. I head over to the secluded patch of sand I've claimed as "my spot" on the beach and unroll my blanket for the last time. My flight out is scheduled for the morning, so I want to soak up every moment of sun and sand and warmth as possible. Which is why I'm a little sad that my afternoon nap ran late. I've just barely made it before the sun sets.

My bag thumps as it falls beside the towel, and I stretch out to a relaxed position. The peace I've known here has been truly sensational. I've FaceTimed my parents every day, keeping up with our normal schedule. But other than that, my phone has been off. I've bonded with random strangers, had moments of clarity with myself, and absolutely no worries of a pop-up from Mary. Pure. Fucking. Heaven.

Waves crashing against the shore and the beautiful sunset sing their own personal lullaby to me. Just as I decide to take nap number two in the open air, I spot a woman walking toward me. I rub my eyes and take a second look; although she's walking in this direction, she can't possibly be walking toward me, as I am hidden by the dune a few yards away.

Maybe she's claimed this area as her spot, too?

Golden skin and red-brown hair are the first things I notice about her before her legs command all my attention. A little too late, I chastise myself and follow her legs up to her determined face. It doesn't look like I'll be convincing her to share, but I lift my hand in a small wave and say hey anyway.

"Hello, mate." Ah, she must be Australian.

Any other thoughts go out the door when she kneels down in front of me and launches right into a kiss.

Well, that's quite the hello, I think to myself, but I'm not complaining. It's been months since I've made out with a girl, what with Mary scheming and blackmailing all the other ladies in our small town to make sure I have no other options but her.

I've been in a desert, and this girl is my first drop of rain. Her soft, curly hair brushes my skin before she grabs my face with both of her small hands. I only get a few more seconds to savor the taste of her before she sits back to look at me.

While her eyes peruse me, I take the opportunity to quickly do the same. She's got a little scar on the left side of her nose. Her heart-shaped face holds beautiful lips that I don't think could ever leave my memory now. And when she looks back up at me, I see the warmest brown eyes; they almost shimmer with gold for a second. Must be the light of the sunset.

As much as I love that a random stranger just came up and kissed the hell out of me, I need to get my head together. She's already looking back down at my lips like she's regretting what just happened, and I can't have that.

"What's your name?" I ask.

"Georshia," she replies. By the tone of her voice, I would almost say she's shy. But her body language looks like she's holding back, and I don't think I could ever call her shy with an introduction like that.

"Georgia?" I confirm. Her eyes pop back up to mine, and I think my heart stops. I'm hit with an overwhelming aroma of pine and sandalwood. Her eyes are bright, and her lips are in an open-mouthed smile. Right then and there, I make a promise to myself to keep her looking like this as long as she'll let me. Even if it's just for today.

"Hi, I'm Lance. Do you always greet people with a kiss?" I smirk, hopefully signaling to her I'm just teasing.

"Only for my mate," she says.

"Okay, so we're friends now?"

"I'd like to be. Very much."

"Well, would you like to continue being 'very much' friends with me?" Oh. My. God. What *the fuck* did I just say?? *See, this is why I'm single.*

I'm about to shove my head into the sand with that stupid line that came straight from my other head when it's like a switch has flipped in Georgia. She shoves my shoulders to the ground and all other words leave my lizard brain.

We're kissing in earnest now—thank god that didn't run her off—and once again, I get a heady whiff of that woodsy aroma that smells so much like home.

Maybe it's a fragrance she's wearing. Even that thought stops when I feel her grinding on me.

My hands go directly to those beautiful red-brown locks as we explore each other's mouths. My girl likes teeth—she's already bit both my tongue and my bottom lip. I can't find it within myself to care.

Georgia must like my reaction because every time my hips jerk up with a graze of her teeth, she hums her appreciation. Her nails dig into my head, my neck, my shoulders, my arms. She's everywhere all at once, and I find I'm welcoming the little pricks of pain she scatters over me. But just when I think I can't take anymore, she breaks off our kiss to look down at me again.

"Unleash yourself." She runs the heel of her palm up my dick.

Yes. Muthafucking. Ma'am. I fumble to pull down my swim shorts while Georgia simply lifts the skirt of her dress. I barely have time to appreciate that she's not wearing any underwear, her gorgeous pussy just suddenly *there*, and, without any preamble, Georgia slams down on me. We both let out a gasp, and, while hers turns into a moan, I think she slammed my brain out somehow. How else can I explain the unadulterated ecstasy I'm feeling right now?

I stare at Georgia for a while, just lost in her beauty, her scent, her warmth, before she moves. *Fuck.*

"You're so beautiful, Georgia," I manage to get out. "You feel so good right now."

With her eyes closed, one hand on my stomach, the other on my thigh, she looks like a ravishing deity coming to bless me with the setting of the sun. I sit up on my elbows just to be closer to her.

She grabs my shoulders for support, bouncing faster on my cock even as her thighs shiver, throwing her head back and mewling softly. It's like a siren call I have to answer. One second, I'm looking at her, and the next, my teeth are on her neck.

Georgia's hands come up to cradle my head, so I don't

feel the need to let go. Her pussy flutters around me, creating a domino effect. My dick throbs stronger than I've ever felt before, causing me to bite down harder on her golden skin. The moment I taste her blood on my tongue, the pressure that's been building in my lower spine suddenly rises.

"Georgia, I *canpullout—*"

"No."

She answers before I can get all the words out. Her head is moving side to side, and her pace has slowed, her breathing ragged. I grab her waist and help her move against me, the both of us barreling toward release.

My hips twitch up with the first intense spurts of cum. I close my eyes then, a feeling of bliss and contentment blanketing me as I lavish Georgia's neck in small licks and kisses. Her pussy continues to contract, and I can feel the shudders working through her body.

I move my kisses up her jaw to her puffy lips. Georgia sighs into my mouth, and I look up to both check in with her and sear this moment into my memory. But when our eyes meet, I see tears in hers.

A cold wrongness comes over my chest, a heavy pit quickly filling my stomach for a moment before she gives me an open-hearted smile, caressing my face with one hand and clutching my arm with the other. I realize they are good tears and that she must be okay, just a little overwhelmed after all that. I lean us back toward the sand to rest for a bit.

CHAPTER 6
GEORGIA

OH. *My. Goddess.*

I'll put out every offering. I'll walk all the way back to the podship to say prayers with Paachzika and Yelena. Anything to keep my mate for the rest of my days. His cock will forever be a beacon beckoning my body and lighting its way back home.

The words for our actions are all flying past me in this language, but I can't even grasp them for fear that I'll take an ounce of attention away from my mate. And just when he shifts forward, pushing deeper inside me, I feel his teeth on my neck a second before everything goes white.

If I hadn't heard omegas talk about what it's like to lie with the alpha, I might've been afraid, but there's no room for fear when my mate accepts our bond by biting me. There are tears in my eyes and on my face when we lift our heads this time.

Lance furrows his eyebrows, and I sense an apprehension in him. With the mating bond still fresh, he must not be able to feel that it's joy spilling out of me, like I can sense his unease. But whatever smile I give him is enough to reassure and straighten out those eyebrows.

With the setting sun at my back and my whole world, my *future*, before me, every worry of not being enough, being hard to manage, being too talkative, goes away. I follow the lines of his face from his slim nose to his hooded eyes back down to those pink lips.

I want to kiss those lips again. They're mine to claim.

But as I lean forward, Lance leans back onto the blanket beneath him. My mate is tired; it seems we will rest for a while.

———

The cool breeze is nothing like the wind and *snow* I saw when we first landed, but everything's better now that I'm with my mate. I can feel his temperature dropping, and I'm afraid my body heat may not be enough for him.

I'm debating whether I should leave him to go find Mazg or wake him up from his beautiful slumber, when my mate stirs. He's like a *sorentas*, a beautiful Yorgürrian river lily that dances in the current, captivating any audience that happens upon it. I can't go anywhere, can't move from this very spot, until I see his deep, brown eyes on me. I run my fingers through his hair to help coax him from his sleep.

With his dick lying hard against his stomach, I have another idea of how to wake him up, but I think that's something we should talk about first.

Soon enough, his beautiful eyes look into mine.

"Hello, mate," I say. My Lance gives me the cutest little just-waking-up grin.

"I was hoping you'd still be here," he says, as if I'd ever willingly leave his side.

"You're cold." I can explain my love for him later; his health is my priority right now.

"Oh, yeah." Lance looks a little sheepish. "I wasn't exactly planning on staying out all night, but what can I say? Earlier, that was... amazing."

"I agree, mate, but we have to get you warm. I just wish —oh! Mazg! Over here!" The boys trail the edge of the beach; they must've been looking for me and Mazg followed my scent here.

A warm spark flutters in my chest at the notion that I made the right decision coming out here with them. If I'd gotten separated from my original pack like this, I know, without a doubt, at least two betas would've intentionally tried to mask the pack's scent so I couldn't find them. Not only do Frank, Johran, and Mazg want to be found, but *they're* coming to find *me*.

Underneath me, I feel my Lance tighten up. "Don't worry, these are my friends."

"Oh. I see." I look down and just barely catch the forlorn look on Lance's face before it's washed away, but I can feel it all the same through our bonds. "I guess you'll be headed back with your friends, then?"

Once he's warm, I'll have more time to explain, but for now, I say, "Of course not! I'm not leaving your side, especially not in your condition. But Mazg is a dragon; he can make us a fire real quick to warm you up."

"Max is a... Wait, what?"

"A dragon," I repeat. Hmph, have I really turned his world upside down like he has mine? "He can usc his belly fire overrr... over there. We'll get you warmed up quick." I stand and reach down to pull him up, but my Lance still has a spacey look on his face as he rights himself just in time to be introduced.

"Mazg, Frank, Johran, this is my mate, Lance. Lance, this is Mazg—a dragon—and Frank and Johran are both—" I pause. "The only equivalent in your language is 'lizards.'" I frown. Back home, their race has a much more esteemed title than what's available here in Lance's tongue.

I glance at the boys for help, but they must not have heard English in the market, so they don't understand yet.

It must not register for Lance because he looks back and forth between the four of us before finally blurting, "Lizard men?!"

"I know it's a rather offensive title, but—"

"You are seriously calling them *lizard men*? Like, that's not a joke? And this guy is a dragon? Please, Georgia, *please* tell me you're joking."

Mazg turns suddenly, directs his orange belly fire to the nearby brush I pointed out earlier, and turns back with a flourish. "Does that answer your question?"

CHAPTER 7
LANCE

I'M MOVING through the airport like a ghost. People give me angry glares as they walk around me, and I'm sure to have my sobriety questioned before I make it home. At this point, I don't care. I've been up literally all night with my three new friends and my... wife—my mate. It still seems so unreal.

I double check my ticket before finding an empty seat near my gate and go over everything all over again. I keep telling myself that the more I repeat it, the more it'll make sense. Hasn't worked yet, but I'm determined to wrap my mind around this.

I'm mated to a wolf. An actual has-fur-and-four-legs-and-howls-at-the-moon wolf. An actual hunts-every-few-nights-a-week-on-four-legs wolf. But not just any regular 'ole wolf in the forest, no. That would be silly. I'm mated to a wolf from outer space! One who shifts into a human with eyes that sometimes shine gold—because *she's a wolf*. One who left her planet, and her pack, to join her friends and look for a better life. Who's friends with a dragon and two lizard men, who are also from outer space.

Aliens.

Aliens are real, and they're here, walking around like everyone else, and I'm *mated* to one.

I turn to look over my shoulders. I know it's silly, but it feels like classified information that I'm going to get arrested just for knowing, for shouting about it in my head.

How do the FBI and CIA agents hold it all in? *Chunk it* —at least, that's what Max told me. Chunk the new information into pieces and only deal with a bit at a time. But finding out your new mate is from... wayyyyyy out of town isn't exactly chunkable. I take a deep breath anyway, and try to move my thoughts along.

Max said that he and twenty-nine other aliens were sent here to wait out their planet's "burn" cycle and that all the aliens are looking forward to trying to find mates while they're here. They've been pumped with different injections to allow them to shift to blend in with humans, and they've even been outfitted with things like the translator chip that allows her and her friends to speak with me.

Georgia explained that she was the runt of her pack, and given the opportunity, she winged it with Max and the twins instead. She also told me I was pronouncing Max's name wrong, but after quite a few tries, he told me it was okay to move on.

It seemed like there was more to that story, and Frank tried to explain, but Max said it would've been too much information for one night. Georgia promised to explain more to me later.

What she made *very clear* was that we are now mated and that, because I bit her, she can feel my emotions through the mating link. Apparently, both mates have to accept the bond before it becomes official, and I did so by biting her. I take a moment just to soak that in. I've never bitten *anyone* before, no matter how good things felt; it's just not normally my thing. So having bitten her at the moment without thought... It feels like this truly is fate and a sign that I'm really meant to be with Georgia with no chance to second guess or mess it up.

And to be honest, she's been nothing but a joy to be around. She's funny, kind, inquisitive, and she enjoys the cold weather like I do. She's the type of person I can be myself around, be vulnerable and honest with. I won't have to hide the fact that I'm well-off behind the struggling artist facade and can just chase my passion freely. Of course, I'll have to introduce her to my parents in baby steps, but I can easily see Georgia and me together. It feels *good.*

This entire ordeal is wild and unbelievable. Almost like it's too good to be true. That someone in the world, or universe rather, aligns so perfectly with me—that we're mates. And then, on top of that, our timelines aligned, and I actually met her.

What if she had been sent to another planet? *Wait,* I can't allow myself to go down that line of thought because that means I have to acknowledge that there are over two planets with living beings on them.

Nope, save that for another day—or better yet, another year.

The transfer of education wasn't one-sided, though. Since Georgia can't get on the plane with me, I had to buy her a cheap travel phone in the downstairs lobby, teach them all how to work a phone, and then teach them how to pull up maps and find me. Johran seemed to catch on to the maps quickly, while Georgia spent an entire hour practicing calling me so, together, I have faith that they have it handled and won't get lost.

Other planes ease down the tarmac when my boarding

group is finally called, and I send up one more prayer for the safety of my new little family to whoever's listening. It's amazing the amount of protection and responsibility I feel for a woman I met less than twenty-four hours ago. We talked about it after the guys left.

"I'm sorry," she whispered in the dark. We were lying in the bed of my hotel room; Georgia the little spoon to my big, and each of us sticking one foot out of the covers on our respective sides.

"Sorry for what?" I asked and eased back her shoulder so she could face me. "What's wrong?"

"I can feel your disdain, your disappointment in me. You don't want me as a mate. You're scared of me."

"What do you mean?" I didn't realize my emotions would be so strong for her and yet so unclear.

"A mate should be both bonded *and* loved, but you don't even know me; how could you love me? You can't want this bond, especially when it's with someone too cowardly to bond back."

"You don't know me either, Georgia, but I'm just as willing to get to know you as you are me. Aliens, exploding planets, mating bonds—this is a lot to take in, but that doesn't make it wrong. *I* bit *you*, Georgia. Without knowing you were my mate, without knowing anything about mating bites. That has to mean something. I know it does."

"Yeah, it means you're stuck with me," she argued. "I'm a beta. I'm basically useless for everything that matters. I can't fight, can't track well; I'll only disappoint you."

I swear I could feel her emotions with the overwhelming guilt and desolation rolling off of her in waves. She could feel my emotions but not read my mind, and I tried to explain that to her.

"No, Georgia—no, mate." I had her attention then. "You

will not disappoint me. I don't need you to hunt or track, you don't even have to do it for yourself unless you want to. You're with me now, in a human body, in a human world. Your pack status only has to mean something to you if *you* want it to. And if you don't like the fact that you're a beta, we can shove it into a box called 'things we don't think about' and let it be."

Georgia rolled onto her stomach and dropped her head onto the pillow beneath her. She lay still for a moment before she turned back to me and whispered, "I don't know who to be if I'm not a beta."

I bit my lip, coasting my hand over her hair and letting out a sigh, trying to see things from her perspective. Reinventing yourself in an unknown world had to be overwhelming for her. Especially when the only family she'd ever known, toxic or not, was still presumably asleep while she was out gallivanting with a mate she'd never thought she'd have.

"You don't have to know who you are or how to be right now. Just make one choice at a time, and pretty soon, you'll fall in love with who you already are."

Georgia gave me another one of her soft smiles. "But you're still scared, though."

I had to smile at her. She was right. I leaned over to kiss her forehead and pull her closer. "I mean, sure, I'm a little scared, but only because your best friend is a dragon." I whispered the last bit conspiratorially to her and looked around as if he might have been hidden in the shadows, which earned me a little giggle.

"I'm scared because I don't know how to protect you. The disdain I have is for a society that already doesn't accept certain humans; how will you possibly be happy here? How will you be happy with me?" I didn't mean to be so vulnerable with her, but it just all tumbled out.

Must've been a good thing though, because she said, "I'll always be happy with you, Lance. Mates aren't just happenstance. Whatever comes our way, we're built to tackle it, together."

And, if nothing else, I proved her claim to be true with my next and probably weakest one-liner yet: "You know what else we can tackle?"

Thank god for a kind and benevolent mate, because she didn't even respond, just swung her leg over and kept me up until checkout.

———

The first thing I do when I land is turn airplane mode off and call Georgia, but they must be flying right now because it goes straight to voicemail. A few moments later, I get check-in texts with a photo of Frank and Johran standing in front of the Las Vegas High Roller. In the photo, Frank gives a wide smile while Johran stares at the camera apathetically. Max had calculated that he would need to take at least one break, so hopefully that will be all he needs and they'll be here soon.

The entire drive home from the airport, I think about what I need to do to prepare for their arrival. The one thing —er, person—I hadn't considered made herself at home while I was away. I already deleted her twenty-eight voice-mails without listening to them after calling my parents while waiting at bag check. Now I'm wishing I listened, if for nothing else than to prepare myself for what I currently see.

Letters stacked on the counter, rose petals on the floor.

She has a "welcome home" poster taped to the wall. She even cleaned out my fridge. Although I'm grateful for her ridding me of the great molder boulder, or Moldie as I'd called him, this has to stop. My mate will be here soon, and while I haven't known her that long, she doesn't seem like the type to laugh something like this off. The only mercy is that Mary isn't here.

The next twenty-five minutes are a blur. Washing laundry, sweeping, mopping, and basically doing anything I can to rid my home of Mary's presence and smell. I throw the last load in when I decide it's time to confront her face-to-face before the gang gets here.

Even though I plan and rehearse what I'm going to say the entire time I walk over to the bakery, I'm still nervous when I pass through the door. I give a few townspeople a nod but don't have to look any further because Mary's already spotted me.

"Welcome home," she says, tucking her pen into her hair. "Did you like your surprises?"

"See, that's actually why I'm here—" I start, but second guess myself. Should I really be giving her the fifth degree in the middle of her workplace?

"Can we go somewhere... quiet?" I immediately regret asking when I see the brief gleam in her eye.

"Lance, you know I'm never quiet."

"Mary, really, it's important." That must get through to her, because she straightens her posture.

"Sure," she says with a small voice, already turning to lead the way. We end up taking a side door that leads back outside by the dumpsters.

"What is it?" she asks as she turns back to me.

Now I see why she flipped her script. The tears in her eyes have stopped an entire conversation between us, but it can't happen this time. My mate's happiness, *my* happiness, and frankly, Mary's safety, depends on it.

"Mary, we've been through this before, but I really need to stress this to you. We're over—"

"Yeah, but—"

"Mary, you broke up with me. Remember? I'm the boring guy who wants to paint and connect to community instead of getting a 'real' job."

"Okay, but I didn't really—"

"Yes, Mary, you *did* mean it that way. And that's okay, because it's the honest truth. And if we stretch our honesty a little bit further, I think you'll find that boredom may be what's motivating you now. Don't give me that face, Mary." I reach to grab her hands in mine because I just can't bear looking at the tears any longer. "This is the same song and dance we've been doing for the last three months. We're no longer together. You have to give me space. Please don't come by my house again unless you're invited."

I wait for her to give me the usual *"But you said your door would always be open?"* retort but instead, she surprises me with downcast eyes. "Okay," she says and lets go of my hands.

"Okay... Okay, well, I'll see you around then, Mary."

"Yeah," she says softly before I turn down the alley and out onto the main street.

As much as I want to believe that she's finally come to her senses, an idea spikes as I pass the hardware store. Hopefully I've got enough time to change a lock or two before my little wolfie gets home.

CHAPTER 8
GEORGIA

MAZG DIPS down for the first time today. We must be close.

I sit in front of Frank and Johran, each of us settled between one of Mazg's translucent, jade-like spikes, so I am the first to see my new home as we duck underneath the clouds. There are pockets and channels of water as far as the eye can see.

Mazg tips to the right, and we pass mountains still covered in snow at the top. I'll have to ask Lance to take me up there. We circle the small town, a cluster of buildings with homes spaced out wide around it, until Mazg makes a sharp left turn. I assume he must have caught Lance's scent and am proven right when we crest a patch of trees and I see the home Lance described to me, every detail as he said. A gray roof tops blue walls with a wooden deck wrapping around the front.

When we touch down in a clearing near Lance's home, my heart feels like it's going to beat right out of my chest. I try, as I have been for the last hour, to decide what I'm going to say to him first.

Do I tell him that I won the bet on who would be more dragon-sick on the way back? Do I tell him about how Mazg made us late because Frank talked him into asking the little machines in Vegas for money and his dragon side wouldn't let him leave without every little gold coin he could get his hands on? And when Johran realized the gold coins were worth real money, it took both me and Frank to tear him away from another machine? Thankfully, since he lost our dragon-sick bet, I made him fork over a third of the winnings. But since they'll be keeping the phone my mate bought me, we felt like it was an equal trade.

"You come find me and let's tackle life together." It's what Lance said the morning he'd left, and every time things get too quiet, the phrase pops back up in my head and scrambles all my thoughts on what I'll say when I see him again.

I have a mate.

One of my own, not shared with a pack.

That thought keeps circling around in my head, and I'm still daydreaming about it and what it means for me when we reach the ground. All of a sudden, it doesn't matter what I say first when I see him, just that I see him.

"Lance! Lance!" I shout as I run. I can hear his footsteps in the home before the door swings open wide, giving me the perfect view of my beautiful mate. Everything about him is just as I remember, but with an extra slice of joy and excitement coming through the bond. Although I almost can't accept what I'm receiving, it's nice to feel the proof that he truly wants me here.

"Georgia! I'm so glad you all made it all right." He scoops me into a hug, waves to everyone, and bear-hug carries me into his home.

Our home.

My first glance takes my breath away. There's wood everywhere, with cushy, fuzzy, and soft textures that remind me of the snow outside. He leads us to the kitchen in the back where he's already set out a meal for us. We try our best to recount the flight back, our smaller pit stops, the word games we played when we weren't sick amongst the clouds, and our full stop in Las Vegas. Pretty soon though, it's time for the boys to leave again. Mazg doesn't want his wings to get too cold, and the sooner they can get out of this climate, the better.

We walk them all the way back to the clearing, and although I'm happy to have found my mate, I realize I'm sad to see my three friends go. This planet feels so big; how long will it be before I see them all again?

"Don't worry, Gjourshe, we'll always be your pack, your *true* pack, along with Lance. We'll visit as often as we can, and we'll use the phones when we can't," Mazg says, reading me like an open book.

"But what about when you're flying?" I whine. I know I'm being a little ridiculous right now, but they're the only other citizens from my home planet who care about me.

"Then you'll just send us a photo like you did with Lance, right? I have to land eventually." He's right, and I say as much.

"Now, go and live your life. And be happy. I can't scent the other wolves anywhere around, but if you see them"—he leans in to whisper—"you know what to do."

I nod and give Mazg one more hug before he shifts into his dragon form. The twins get their last hugs too, although I'm sure Johran would've been fine with just a nod and a wave, and then they are off.

Lance puts his arm around me after we can't see them anymore. "Ready to go home?"

"As a matter of fact, I am."

CHAPTER 9
GEORGIA

ONCE MY NEW pack is gone, Lance washes the dishes. He instructed me to wash up and relax from the trip, but I have other plans. We told him *almost* everything about our stop in Vegas during dinner, but I can thank Frank's recklessness and Mazg's embarrassment for the surprise I've got planned next for Lance.

Late in the Vegas evening, we looked for a place to spend the night and were asking around when someone recommended a store to us. Frank's curiosity won out, and we perused the small store with blacked-out windows and red lights. Now I grab my purchases from my small pack and head to the bathroom.

In the shower's steam, I wash both my body and the toys. Everything came with a full charge, but I plug them in on the counter to top them off while I try to make sense of my wet curls.

As a wolf, and a beta at that, I've never been too concerned with how my fur stuck up every which way, as long as it was clean. Now, in this human body, I'll need to pay more attention to grooming trends here.

For now, I run my fingers through my hair a few times until it's all going in the same direction, falling toward my back. I grab a towel off the rack and realize I didn't bring that lacy fabric in here with me. I glance at my naked body in the mirror and shrug; I'll save it for next time.

Lance is back in the bedroom by the time I leave the bathroom. I'm so distracted from the scent of my mate that I forget to hide my new toys behind my back.

"Georgia," Lance says slowly. "What are those?"

I grin. "They're our new toys, a mating present for both of us." I hold them in front of me proudly, with open hands. "Do you like them?"

Lance peruses the collection of cock rings, vibrators, and one silver butt plug, amongst other silicone and leather items. "I'm honestly not sure what half of this is, but I'm excited to try them."

Good enough for me!

"Shall we start with this one, then?" I hold up the blue cock ring, and Lance's smiling nod is all the go ahead I need. I set the others down on the nightstand as Lance walks around to meet me. But our lips meet like magnets, and the ring is temporarily forgotten on the bed while I taste my mate's soft lips for the first time in two days.

My hands go into his hair, and he grips my hips as we sway in our kiss. Lance dips his tongue into my mouth and moans when I suck on it. It's not long before my teeth get involved, and his tiny little grunts and groans and the quick snaps of his hips push me to keep things going.

A simple tug on his joggers makes him just as nude as I am, and then I'm wrapping my leg around him while trying to pull his face impossibly closer.

"I missed you, mate," I say against his lips. My voice

sounds huskier than I intend, but it portrays my need for Lance all the same.

He gives me two quick kisses before backing up to pull out a drawer in his nightstand. "I missed you too, baby." He produces a bottle from the drawer and hands it over to me. "Do you know what this is, Georgia?"

I shake my head no, watching him pop open the top and waft it under my nose. "This is lube. Humans use this to help keep things slick. We especially use it with toys, since most aren't self-lubricating. Will you put it on me and then the ring?"

I hold my hand out for him to pour some in my palm, and then I massage his cock with one hand and reach for the c-ring with the other. The royal blue looks beautiful against his hard, veiny cock. The Vegas sales associate had explained that the top half goes around his cock while the bottom goes around his balls. And with a little help from Lance, we get it in place.

Lance lowers onto the bed, pulling me with him so I'm straddling his legs. He gives himself two pumps before lifting my chin so that I'm looking him in the eyes.

"What next, mate?" he asks.

I'm ready to tell him, but when I open my mouth, all that comes out is a moan on account of him tracing a line up my neck with his tongue.

"I was hoping you... would tell me," I finish on a sigh.

"Oh?" Lance says before repeating his tracing on the other side. I shiver, both from the heat of his tongue and the nerves of what I'm about to confess.

"Yes, I need—I need you to dominate me, mate." Lance stops his perusal to look me in the eye. "I need you to rut me, uhm, and—" and I'm probably asking for too much.

"And?" my mate prompts. I search the bond before I

continue, but all I find is what I can already see in his eyes: fire, focus, passion.

"And I want to seal our bond. I want you to rut me here." I place my hand on my butt. "Your language calls it doggy style and..." I have to laugh. "I'm not sure how I feel about that yet."

Lance and I share a smile, and he wraps his arms around me. "Sweetie, we can call it whatever you want. What else?"

"That's it."

Lance kisses me. "Are you sure?"

"Yes." Another kiss.

"And I'm in charge?"

"Yes." This kiss lasts a little longer, giving me time to savor the feeling of heat pooling at my core before I'm thrown into the air, arms reaching, heart reeling, and twisted to land with my back on the bed. My Lance has been hiding a secret talent. I quite like being thrown around, and I tell him as much.

"Then let me see this pretty pussy, Georgia. Are you ready to be devoured?"

"Yes," I answer again, a lot more breathless than before. My eyes track him placing a pillow behind my head, but otherwise, I don't move an inch. I don't know where this side of Lance has been hiding, but I hope it sticks around. Lance lowers slowly to his knees, kissing the inside of my thighs on the way down, his eyes never leaving mine. The first swipe of his tongue on my clit causes my head to fly back and my hips to roll.

"Little wolfie," my mate singsongs to me, "this is your one and only warning. When you break eye contact"—he drags his tongue flat against me again—"this stops. Do you understand?"

I nod. "Yes."

"Good, now show me how you touch those breasts when you think of me," he says, leaving me blinking at him for a moment. Once he sees my hands move to follow his instructions, he resumes his mission. His large hands skim over my skin, stopping underneath my knees to hold me more open.

"You're so fucking beautiful, Georgia." I almost don't hear him, even though he's looking right at me, because he says it so quietly to himself.

He lowers his head back down, and the next touch I feel is at that sensitive button at the apex of my pussy, his mouth and tongue both licking and kissing, his eyes promising, and my brain quickly flatlining. I get lost in the sensations he wrings out of me now.

Soon, he flicks my clit with his fingers before deep diving those fingers into my pussy and focusing his mouth on kissing and licking my rosebud below. Time passes both too slowly and yet not slow enough as I'm once again brought to the edge of the world.

"Let me hear you. Let me hear my mate scream for me."

That does it. My orgasm comes in waves that temporarily unmoor me from reality. I twitch and fidget, not completely in control of my limbs, and try to focus on breathing. Lance is still lapping at me, and I focus on his hands and tongue on my body to ground me.

"Little wolfie," Lance calls me again when I can see straight. "Are you ready for me to rut you?"

"Yes," I whisper.

"Attagirl. Turn around for me." He doesn't even wait for me to try moving before picking me up and gently flipping me over. "Beautiful."

He moves the pillow from its current home, caught under my shoulder, and adjusts it under my hips.

"You still with me, mate?" he asks.

I'm about to retort that I don't know what would give him the idea that I'm not. But then I picture what I must look like to him, a strung out and boneless starfish on his bed, and give a yes that sounds more like, "Mphah," with my face buried in the sheets.

His hands trace my ass and legs, then up to my back.

"Good. Count me down, Georgia." He drags his dick along my seam as he speaks.

He lifts my hips and sets them back down where he wants them. "One."

"One," I repeat back, having turned my head to breathe easier.

"Two."

"Tuh!" I shout as he slams into my pussy.

"That's right," he says. "Let me hear you unravel."

Those same snapping movements I loved so much when I teased him are now back with a vengeance. Lance slams into me over and over, somehow both slow and powerful. All I can do is moan.

Lance continues to play my body like an instrument, adjusting my hips, pulling me back before I reach the edge of the bed, changing the angle to make me feel new things before, all of a sudden, his deep thrusts become shallow. I whip my head around to see that he's already looking at me. The serious, determined look on his face tells me everything I need to know.

He pulls out his cock and replaces it with two fingers. "A mate should be bonded." His fingers glaze my rose. "A mate should be loved. A mate should be rutted." He pushes one, then both fingers in. "Don't you agree?"

I pause, thinking he's going to move quickly like before, but all he does is slowly move those fingers in and out, that look of quiet determination still in place.

"Yes," I respond.

"Yes, what?"

"Yes, mate... A mate should be rutted."

"Oh, well then, Georgia," he says with a playful half-smile, "you may want to hold on."

I barely have time to register his words and grab hold of the sheets before he's slammed back into me in a whole new way. And he doesn't stop. Over and over, Lance ruts into me with a passion and vigor I can feel brightly through our bond. I'm grounded by his soft kisses to my neck and shoulder, a complete contradiction of what's happening in my most intimate parts.

All I can do is moan my appreciation.

"Little wolfie." He halts his hips for a few seconds to take the c-ring off. "Give me what I need."

With his cock back in me and his mouth tracing my neck, I let go completely, shattering underneath him. Drowning in the bliss of our completed bond.

Under the currents, I swear I can feel our hearts knitting together, two pieces of one whole, unseverable. I'm crying again. And for the first time, I know what it's like to truly belong to someone. To matter.

The heat of his cum bathing my insides mirrors the heat in my chest, a physical marker of what we've done, the commitment we've made to each other.

Lance slows and lowers down to me, weaving our fingers together in a loose handhold and turning us onto our sides. We both lie there for a while, just breathing and enjoying this new sensation. He kisses my hair and my neck and my shoulder. I fall asleep with my whole world in my hands.

————

The sun isn't fully up yet when I hear rustling outside. My mate sleeps soundly beside me, so I make the executive decision to snuggle into him and ignore it, focusing on the melodic rhythm of his deep breathing and soft snores. A few minutes later though, I hear the same persistent rustling again, and it sounds like it's right outside the back door. I take a deep breath and slowly inch out of bed so as not to wake up my mate.

At the bottom of the stairs, an offensive smell sits heavy in my nostrils.

Female.

And that's when it hits me. I connect her rose water scent with the fading scent on Lance's couch and dining table. She's been here before.

Oh, hell no.

This is my territory now. My woods. My house. My man, my man, my man.

My first instinct is to tear down the door and tear into her ass, but I'm on a new planet now with new rules. Out the window, I spot her, and it seems like she's looking for something. I just can't fathom what she might be looking for in my mate's backyard.

Her sanity, maybe?

"Can I help you?" I ask as I swing open the door. The frightened squeak she gives is one hundred percent worth the dramatics. "Why are you here?"

"Who are you?" she asks with a furrow in her brow that tells me she thinks she's entitled to an answer. She thinks this is her space, not mine. While I won't begrudge my mate relationships before I got here, now that I'm here, I'll be the only one. And she needs to understand that.

"I ask the questions here," I say as I stalk toward her. "You're on my property, and when I—"

"*Your* property?"

"—ask a question, I expect it to be answered, so I'll ask it again. Who. Are. You?" I punctuate each word with the three steps it takes to close the distance between us. She gasps and stammers before her eyebrows raise almost to her hairline and then slam back down.

"I'm Lance's girlfr—"

"No, you're not."

"Yes, I—"

"No, you're not." I don't know when my face got close enough to hers for our foreheads to touch, but I'm certainly not backing up now. "And if you didn't know it before, you know now. You are not Lance's girlfriend. And I know this because I am his mate. His love. His wife. His sun and moon. I'm it for Lance, just as he is for me."

I take a breath, and she's smart enough not to interrupt again, so I continue, "So when I tell you to get off my property and not return, trust that Lance will not come to your rescue should I need to remove you myself. Now stop stinking up my backyard so I can get back to *snuggling with my mate.*"

Her mouth closes to form a pout, and I think for a moment she might try to say something else, but her survival skills win out, and she turns to leave. I scoop up the package she must have brought and take it inside. Blueberry muffins, my new favorite.

CHAPTER 10

LANCE

YOU KNOW those dreams that feel hyper-realistic, but you deny something could be wrong so you can get more sleep, only to wake up and realize that something *was* actually wrong? That's how I ended up falling out of bed with this seething need to protect and defend in my chest. In my confusion, I get tangled in the bedsheets and step on a remote, trying to get to the door. I snatch a pair of sweatpants off the floor and head downstairs.

I know immediately what spurned that feeling when I reach the bottom of the stairs to see Georgia walking through the back door with a basket—Mary's basket. She must've seen the basket and gotten a whiff of Mary's perfume that always clings to the ribbon on the handle. Better to explain to her now than later.

"Hey, Georgia."

"Hello, mate." She looks up at me with such serenity in her eyes before popping a blueberry muffin into her mouth.

"Those blueberry muffins are from a girl in town," I begin.

"I know," she states, mouth half full. That would make

sense; she can probably tell that the basket and its owner are from the area just on scent alone.

"They're from a girl named Mary," I continue. "We used to date, but we broke up months ago, and I told her to stay away."

"Oh, Mary." Georgia drags her name out like she's trying out the sounds for the first time, her eyes going distant before zeroing in on her next blueberry victim. "It's good to know her name."

"You're not mad that she came around?" I ask timidly.

Her head snaps in my direction and Georgia gives me a 1000-watt smile. "Mad? Of course not! In pack culture, it is in bad taste to kill someone without knowing their name, and you've just given it. If she doesn't heed the warning I've given her, I'm well within my rights to carve out her throat with my claws and eat it for dinner... with a side of these blueberry muffins."

Oooo-kay.

Georgia pops another into her mouth, and I question if she's even chewing them. But then I circle back to what she just said now that the surprise of her lethal tone has worn off.

"Wait, so you met her? Did you see her when she dropped off the muffins? You can't kill her, Georgia; you'd go to jail, and we'd be separated. And seriously, aren't you going to share? I'm hungry too." All of my questions tumble out before I can catch them, and Georgia blinks at me once, twice, before drifting the basket of muffins within my reach. I snag one quickly before she changes her mind.

"I know she can be a nuisance. Really, I do. But let's not go killing people unless they harm us first. Can we agree to that?"

Georgia stops chewing and stands up, making the chair she sat in fall backward. "But you've been hurt."

"What do you mean?" I look down just to check, but all the bruises and bite marks I see were well-earned last night.

"I can feel it through the bond: you're nervous, scared, and to me, that's as good as hurt."

"I *am* scared, Georgia, but not because of her. I felt this seething rage in my sleep, a strong need to protect, to fight. It's what woke me up just now. I was afraid because it felt like a heart attack or something. When I first came down here, I thought it was your emotions, but you looked so calm and peaceful that now I'm worried that it *was* a heart attack and, worse yet, that something went wrong last night. What if the bond didn't work? Why can't I feel you?"

I move to sit down, but Georgia stops me, putting her arms around me, an ear to my chest.

"Oh, my mate." She looks up at me. "Your heart is just fine. You were right, it was my emotions you felt at first, but when you came down the stairs, well, it's hard to feel murderous when I'm looking at you. I accepted the mate bond with you last night, officially, when you rutted me... better than any wolf ever could." She smirks then, likely feeling what her words are doing to me against her stomach.

"You have a direct line to my heart now, as I do to yours. Close your eyes and try to quiet your mind. Can you feel me now? The joy you give me just by existing?"

Oh. Yeah, I can feel her joy, all right, and her insatiable hunger too. I grip her hair and pull her head back to kiss her and see if we can ignore the morning sun for a few more hours when my phone rings. Somehow, I forgot it was Wednesday.

"It's my parents. Are you ready to meet them?" I ask her

instead. I have already explained to Georgia my mom's condition and how important routine is for people with dementia. It's nine a.m. in North Carolina, and she'll be getting ready to go to bingo soon, so it's the best time for mom to learn new information or people. I know I can count on dad to help by repeating things to her throughout the day.

Georgia's smile and the love and affection I now recognize as her emotions through the bond are all the answers I need, and we both rush upstairs before it goes to voicemail. Before I swipe to answer, though, I remind her, "Just no talk about your previous planet yet, okay?"

The look she gives when she says, "Of course not," has me hoping for strength.

GEORGIA

THE MORNING GREETS me with robin calls and calm breezes. It's hard to know day from night now with twenty-four-hour daylight, but Lance and I have kept to the same schedule every day to prepare for his parents flying in today, so it should be about seven a.m..

I glance at the clock just to confirm, because I've made that mistake before, and then turn over to gaze at my beautiful mate, my first and favorite part of my morning routine. I slide his hair out of his face before taking in his eyebrows and jaw, his neck and chest, and his v lines that lead to his morning wood. At least the two of *us* are awake. Which reminds me to check his wrists.

I think I'm out of luck when I see his bare right arm, but his left wrist and hand are concealed beneath his pillow. The little brat, he probably did that on purpose. I turn my body toward him so that I can ease one corner of the pillow up ever so slightly. I almost laugh out loud with glee when I see the blue scrunchie on his left wrist. My green light.

I pull the sheets down and kneel over him, every movement soft and quiet so as not to wake him until the big reveal. It takes a bit of effort to move my side-sleeper mate into position, but soon enough, I'm moving down to lick his hips and stomach, careful not to let my teeth get involved and ruin the fun.

I drag the flat of my tongue along the bottom of his cock to gauge where he is in his sleep cycle. Lance lets out a breath but is otherwise still sound asleep. Time to change that. I take his entire cock into my mouth to get it wet and then grip and twist with my hand while I move my mouth to his balls.

After eighteen months together, we're both ready and excited to conceive a child, so I massage his little swimmers real good. Lance said that if we have the baby in winter, I will get to pick the name, but if it's a summer baby, he's going to choose. Either way, our child will borrow the name of one of Lance's elders, becoming their *atiq*. We're not exactly sure how long a cross-species pregnancy will take, even with my human-like body, so at this point, I'm just crossing my fingers that they're healthy and happy when they get here.

Lance's head is moving side to side a little, and his legs start to tense and release, so I know he'll be waking up soon. I shift forward and balance one hand on his stomach to impale myself on his dick with the other.

My head falls back immediately in response to our connection. Everything is right in the world when I'm one with my mate. I'm rocking softly back and forth, musing over that claim when I realize I may have to amend it.

Lance's chocolate brown eyes open and land on me, and I smile to myself.

Everything is right in the world when my mate looks at me like I'm the only thing that matters.

"Hello, mate." I drag my nails up and down his chest

and stomach, reveling in his small clenches and jerks that show me just how much I affect him. I'm almost hypnotized by how his body reacts to mine, so much so that when Lance quickly grabs my hips and flips us over, I feel like I just experienced a mini tornado, completely unawares.

"Hello, little wolfie," he whispers softly into my ear.

I whisper back, "Breed me, Lance," and smile when I turn my head to see the look in his eyes. Today's going to be a good day.

WANT MORE?

For bonus content (including what happened in Vegas) and first looks at what's coming next in the series, click here:

Join the chaos cuties

ACKNOWLEDGMENTS

Oh my God. Oh my God. It's the end of the book! Okay, don't freak out, breathe, *breathe.* *exhale* I CAN'T BELIEVE YOU JUST READ MY BOOK!!!

I am so thoroughly and utterly grateful to you for giving me and my little wolfie a chance. I can't express how heartwarming but also mind-numbing it is to actually achieve my dream of publishing a book. Like, is this real life?

There's no way in the world that I could have gotten here without my mom (WHO IS ONLY ALLOWED TO READ THIS **ONE** PAGE IN THE ENTIRE BOOK) and the constant support of my Fab Five. You all give me a soft place to land in the worst of times, and a belly full of laughter in the best of times. A big hug and thank you to my Grampie for putting up with my shenanigans and Leo behavior, and my Grammie, my first teacher, who isn't here but always is. I love you all.

I also want to thank my fellow writers DM Lewery, Ashleigh Logan, and Leigha Wilkins as well as some of my biggest cheerleaders Sarah, JD, Liz, Ruthie, and Karissa. You all have encouraged and empowered me, and didn't let me give up on myself. Your kindness means so much to me.

I also owe a huge shout out to Clio Evans; without their Creature Cafe series, this book wouldn't exist. Thank you for boldly writing your stories, you taught me how to be brave. Thank you to Alessa Thorn (ohmigod I would die if she read this), your books have helped me weather many a storm, both physical and mental. Thank you to Katee Robert, Amy Kuivalainen, Molly Tullis, and Rachel Alexander, you all inspire me every day.

Lastly, thank you to YOU! Thank you for supporting a five year old with grabby hands in the library, a preteen hiding her feelings behind pages, a young adult scared to step out of society's rigid box, and a woman who's only just found her voice. I hope this book, in some way, strengthened yours.

ABOUT WHIT LAVONNE

Whit is a romance and fantasy reader and writer living in Detroit and probably dreaming about the beach. She loves Marvel, dogs, and all things theater. Her favorite travel destination so far has been Cuba and her favorite job has been working attractions at Disney World. She teaches 6th grade students how to write the best theme sentences this world has ever seen and her most ordered take out meal is chicken tikka masala.

You can learn more here:
https://linktr.ee/heyitswhitlavonne

www.ingramcontent.com/pod-product-compliance
Lightning Source LLC
Chambersburg PA
CBHW060508300726
48975CB00008B/2704